W9-CDD-769

On Market Street

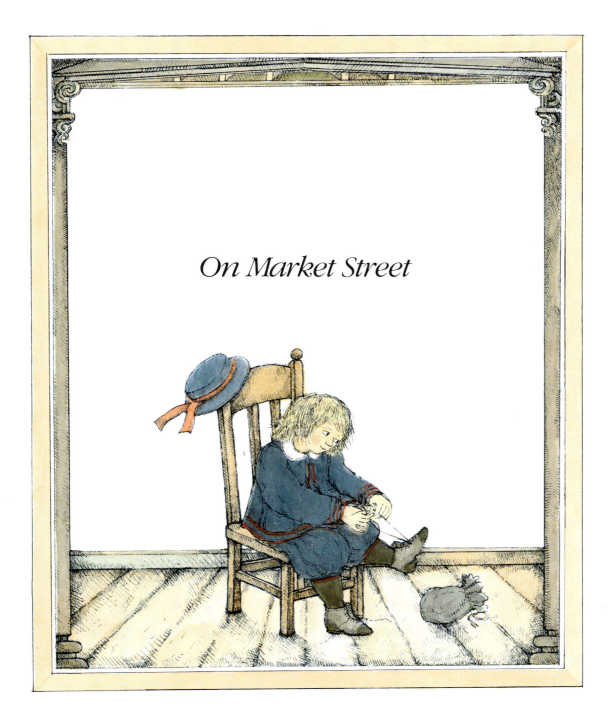

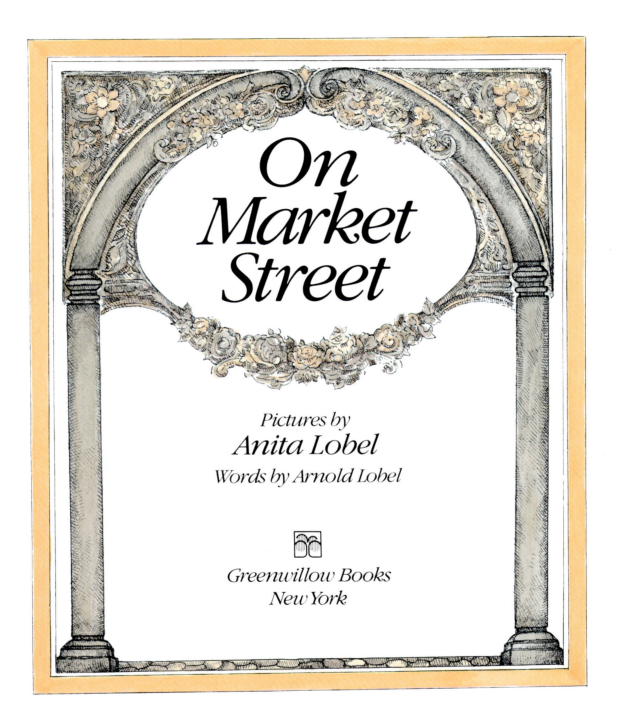

On Market Street

Pictures by
Anita Lobel

Words by Arnold Lobel

Greenwillow Books
New York

Library of Congress Cataloging-in-Publication Data   Lobel, Arnold.   On Market Street.
"Greenwillow Books."
Summary: A child buys presents from A to Z in the shops along Market Street.
[1. Shopping—Fiction. 2. Alphabet 3. Stories in rhyme.]   I. Lobel, Anita.   II. Title.
PZ8.3.L820m   [E]   80-21418   ISBN 0-688-80309-1
ISBN 0-688-84309-3 (lib. bdg.)   ISBN 0-688-08745-0 (paper)

To Timothy and Susan Benn

The merchants down on Market Street
Were opening their doors.
I stepped along that Market Street,
I stopped at all the stores.
Such wonders there on Market Street!
So much to catch my eye!
I strolled the length of Market Street
To see what I might buy.

And I bought…

apples,

B

books,

clocks,

D

doughnuts,

E

eggs,

flowers,

G

gloves,

hats,

I

ice cream,

jewels,

K

kites,

lollipops,

M

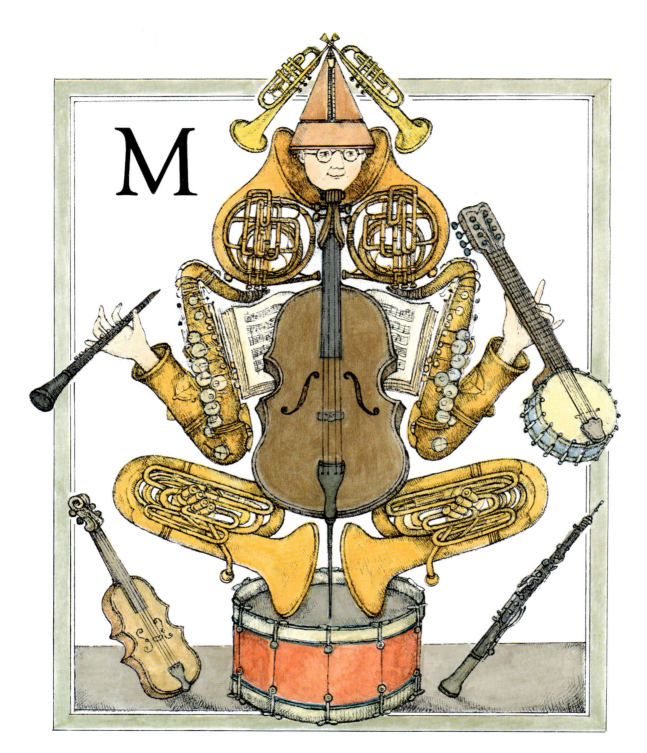

musical instruments,

noodles,

oranges,

P

playing cards,

quilts,

ribbons,

S

shoes,

toys,

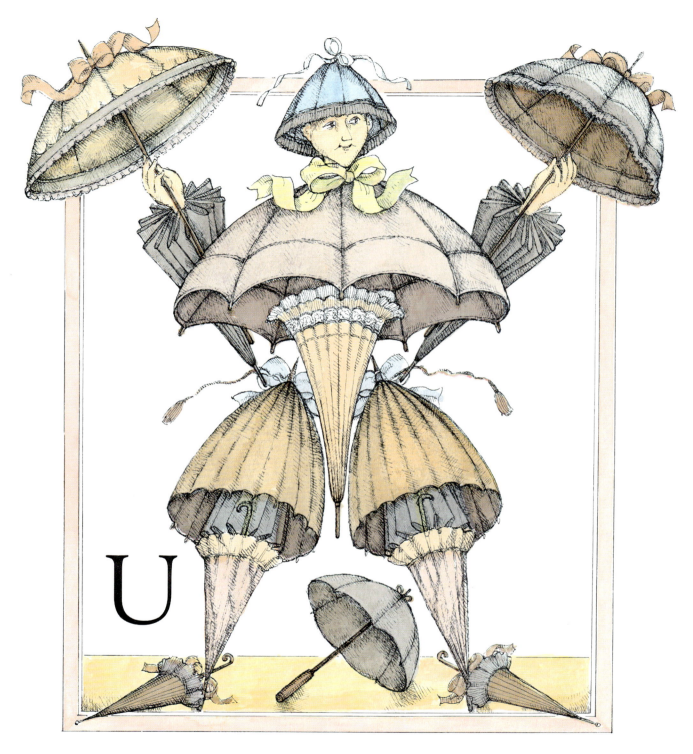

U

umbrellas,

V

vegetables,

W

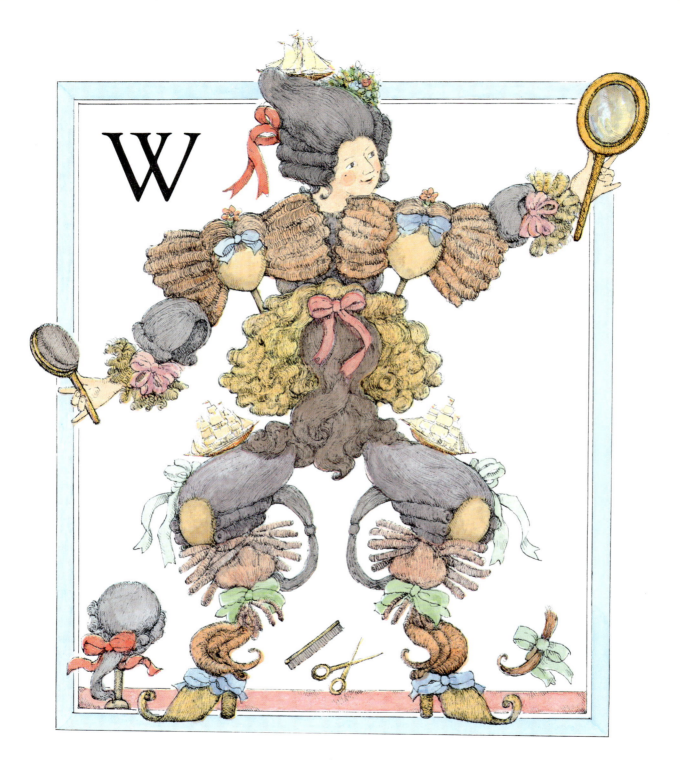

wigs,

Xmas trees,

yarns,

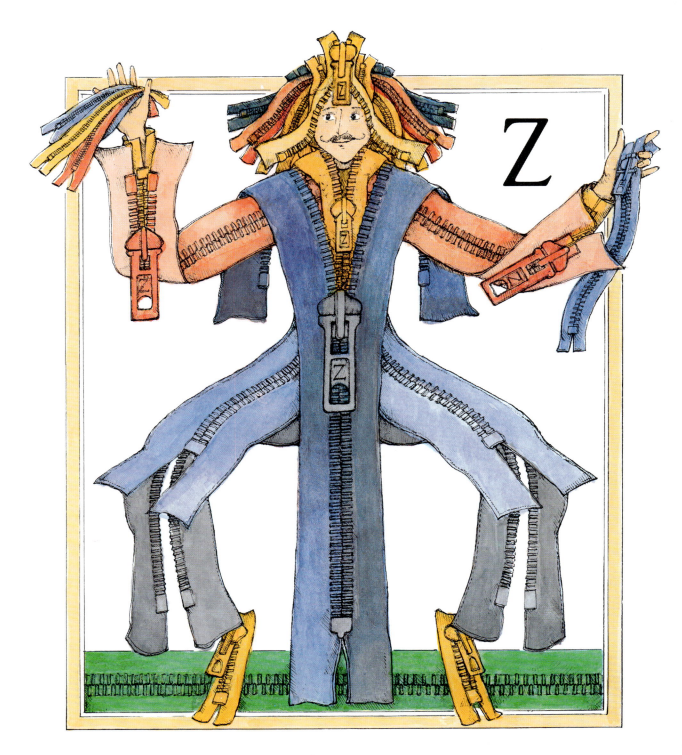

zippers.

My arms were full on Market Street,
I could not carry more.
As darkness fell on Market Street,
My feet were tired and sore.
But I was glad on Market Street,
These coins I brought to spend,
I spent them all on Market Street...

…on presents for a friend.

Anita and *Arnold Lobel*,
after many years as separate
artistic entities, say that there is
great joy in collaboration.
The first book on which they
joined their talents was <u>How
the Rooster Saved the Day</u>. This
was followed by <u>A Treeful of
Pigs</u>, an ALA Notable Book. <u>On
Market Street</u> was inspired
by the Children's Book Week
poster which Anita Lobel
created in 1977.